FUNNY-SIDE UP

A SpongeBob Joke Book

© 2014 Viacom International Inc. All rights reserved. Published in the United States by Random House Children's Books, a division of Random House LLC, a Penguin Random House Company, 1745 Broadway, New York, NY 10019, and in Canada by Random House of Canada Limited, Toronto. Originally published as three separate titles by Simon & Schuster, Inc.: *Funny-Side Up*, in 2009; *Jokes from the Krusty Krab*, in 2005; and *SpongeBob JokePants*, in 2002. Random House and the colophon are registered trademarks of Random House LLC. Nickelodeon, SpongeBob SquarePants, and all related titles, logos, and characters are trademarks of Viacom International Inc.

created by

Stephen Hillenburg

randomhouse.com/kids

ISBN 978-0-385-37432-3

Printed in the United States of America

10 9 8 7 6 5 4 3 2

FUNNY-SIDE UP

A SpongeBob Joke Book

By Chip Eliot
and
David Lewman

Random House 🏠 New York

Are you ready to navigate through the SpongeBob SquarePants joke zone?

How does SpongeBob like his eggs?

Funny-side up.

Why did Patrick hold a stone and a Krabby Patty bun to his ears?

He wanted to hear some rock and roll.

SpongeBob: Patrick, will you join me in a cup of ice-cold lemonade?

Patrick: No, I don't think there's room for both of us.

Why did SpongeBob bring a tub of margarine to Mrs. Puff?

He was trying to butter her up.

Why couldn't the egg lend Patrick any money?

Because it was broke.

What happened when SpongeBob ate one plate of spaghetti too many?

He went pasta point of no return.

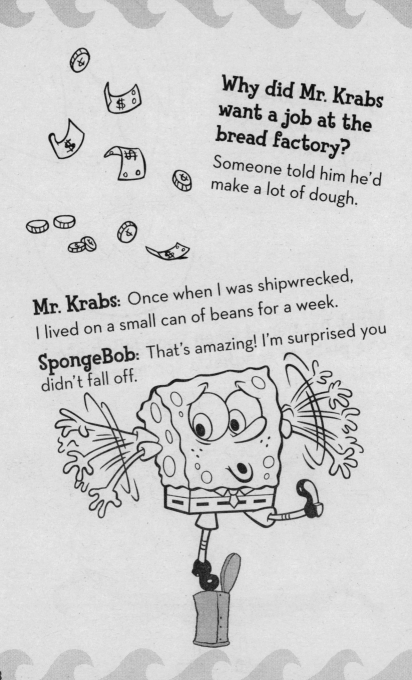

Why did Mr. Krabs want a job at the bread factory?

Someone told him he'd make a lot of dough.

Mr. Krabs: Once when I was shipwrecked, I lived on a small can of beans for a week.

SpongeBob: That's amazing! I'm surprised you didn't fall off.

Mr. Krabs: Try some of my seaweed salad. It will put some color in your cheeks.

Sandy: Who wants green cheeks?

Patrick: I'll have a Krabby Patty, Mr. Krabs.

Mr. Krabs: With pleasure.

Patrick: No, with tartar sauce.

What is Squidward's favorite fruit?

Sour grapes.

Squidward: Mr. Krabs, how do you make a gold-medal Krabby Patty?

Mr. Krabs: Easy. Just add fourteen carrots.

Patrick: Why is my Krabby Patty all squished?

SpongeBob: You told me you were in a hurry and that I should step on it.

Why does Squidward complain whenever he eats?

He likes to whine and dine.

Mrs. Puff: I'd like a Krabby Patty, and make it lean.

SpongeBob: Which way?

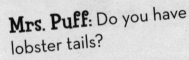

Mrs. Puff: Do you have lobster tails?

Mr. Krabs: Yes, once upon a time, there was a little lobster . . .

Mrs. Puff: What fruit can you find everywhere in the ocean?

Pearl: That's easy. Currants.

Why did SpongeBob study all the old grease stains left on the grill at the Krusty Krab?

Mrs. Puff said he should learn about ancient Greece.

Why did Patrick swallow a bunch of coins?

His mother said it was lunch money.

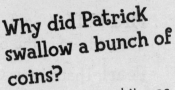

What did SpongeBob say when he saw the brand-new griddle at the Krusty Krab?

"Ah, the grill of my dreams!"

Pearl: What kind of cup can't you drink out of?

Patrick: A cupcake.

Why did Patrick toss a peach into the air?

He wanted to see a fruit fly.

Mrs. Puff: What is this fly doing in my alphabet soup?

Mr. Krabs: Learning to read?

Patrick: This Krabby Patty is way too rare. Didn't you hear me say well done?

Squidward: Yes, I did. Thank you very much.

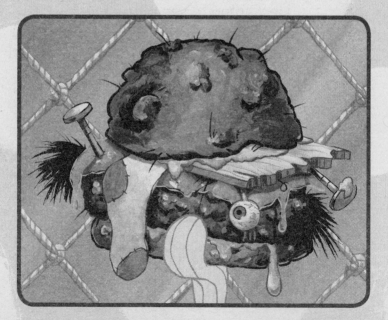

What do sailors like to eat for lunch in Bikini Bottom?

Submarine sandwiches.

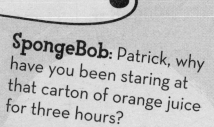

SpongeBob: Patrick, why have you been staring at that carton of orange juice for three hours?

Patrick: It says "Concentrate"!

How did Mr. Krabs learn to cook?

He took ten greasy lessons.

Patrick: SpongeBob, can you fix dinner?

SpongeBob: I didn't even know it was broken.

Mr. Krabs: How was your chicken soup?

Sandy: It was fowl.

Plankton: Do you take orders to go?

SpongeBob: Yes.

Plankton: Well, then—GO!

Why did SpongeBob put a chicken in his garden?

He was trying to grow eggplant.

Why did SpongeBob take a Krabby Patty bun to a fashion show?

He wanted it to be a roll model.

What happened when Pearl won the Bikini Bottom hot-dog-eating contest?

She was declared the wiener.

Sandy: How long will my Krabby Patty be?

Mr. Krabs: It won't be long. It will be round.

Sandy: What kind of shoes can you make from bananas?

Patrick: I don't know.

Sandy: Slippers.

Who brings candy to all the good boys and girls in Bikini Bottom in the spring?

The Oyster Bunny.

Why did Sandy put sugar under her pillow?

She wanted to have sweet dreams.

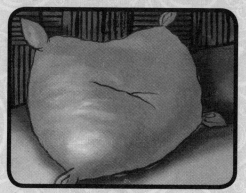

Why did Patrick quit his job at the doughnut factory?

He was sick of the "hole" business.

Pearl: Why is it impossible to starve on a beach?

Sandy: Because of all the sand which is on it.

What does King Neptune like to drink?

Royal tea.

Why did Patrick put a frankfurter in the freezer?

He wanted a chilly dog.

What does a pirate have in common with corn that costs a dollar?

Both are a buck an ear.

SpongeBob: Did you hear about the egg that laughed itself silly?

Patrick: No, what happened?

SpongeBob: It cracked up!

SpongeBob: What do astronauts put on their sandwiches?

Sandy: Launch meat.

Where can you see hamburgers dance?

At a meatball.

Patrick: What is your stew like today?

Mr. Krabs: Just like last week's, only a week older.

Was Squidward mad when SpongeBob jumped on his mop?

Yes, he flew off the handle.

Why couldn't Plankton pay for his Krabby Patty?

He was a little short.

What side order does Sandy always get with her Krabby Patty?

Squirrelly fries.

What does SpongeBob do when Squidward drops food?

He goes on a mopping spree!

What does Mr. Krabs like best about SpongeBob?

His buckteeth.

How does Mr. Krabs start every bedtime story?

"Once upon a dime . . ."

What's Mr. Krabs's favorite kind of bread?

Pumper-nickel.

What kind of nuts does Mr. Krabs like the best?

Cash-ews.

What do you see when Mr. Krabs's daughter smiles?

Her Pearly whites.

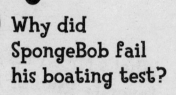

Why did SpongeBob fail his boating test?

He forgot to fasten his sea belt.

Mrs. Puff: Knock-knock.

SpongeBob: Who's there?

Mrs. Puff: Teach.

SpongeBob: Teach who?

Mrs. Puff: Teach yourself to drive—I give up!

RULES of the ROAD

What does every restaurant get when SpongeBob's behind the wheel?

A drive-through.

Patrick: What do sponges play at their birthday parties?

SpongeBob: Musical squares.

What game does SpongeBob play with his shoes?

Hide-and-squeak.

Why did SpongeBob tear himself in half at the end of the party?

Because Sandy said it was time to split.

Why did SpongeBob wash the reef?

He was practicing good coral hygiene.

Is Plankton nice to the reefs around Bikini Bottom?

No, he's rotten to the coral.

How do angelfish greet each other?

"Halo!"

Why does Sandy's fur stand up on end whenever Plankton's around?

He rubs her the wrong way.

Where do Sandy and SpongeBob practice their karate?

In choppy water.

Sandy: What kind of pizza do they serve at the bottom of the ocean?

SpongeBob: Deep-dish.

What kind of earrings does Sandy's mom wear?

Mother-of-squirrel.

What do you get when you cross a squid and a dog?

An octo-pooch.

What do you get when you cross a hunting dog, a seagull, and a bumblebee?

A bee-gull.

Why can't Sandy play on Patrick's basketball team?

Because he's on an all-star team.

Why did Patrick stare at a mirror with his mouth open?

Squidward told him to watch his tongue.

What's salty and feels good on a sunburn?

The Pacific Lotion.

SPF 45

Is Patrick happy with the way he looks?

Yes, he's tickled pink!

What makes Patrick grouchy?

Waking up on the wrong side of the rock.

Why did SpongeBob chop the joke book in half?

Squidward told him to cut the comedy.

What's the most popular hobby in Bikini Bottom?

Damp-collecting!

How did Squidward do in the hundred-yard dash?

He won by a nose.

What kind of ocean bird can't fly, can't swim, and can't catch fish?

A peli-can't.

What did SpongeBob yell when he dressed up as a bear?

"I'm Teddy!"

Squidward: Why does Gary meow?

SpongeBob: Because he doesn't know how to bark!

SpongeBob: What does food start out as?

Sandy: Baby food.

SpongeBob: What kind of food do you feed to sharks with your bare hands?

Squidward: Finger food.

When is food like Plankton?

When it goes bad.

SpongeBob: Why do fishermen like to fish where there are tons of mosquitoes?

Sandy: 'Cause they get lots of bites!

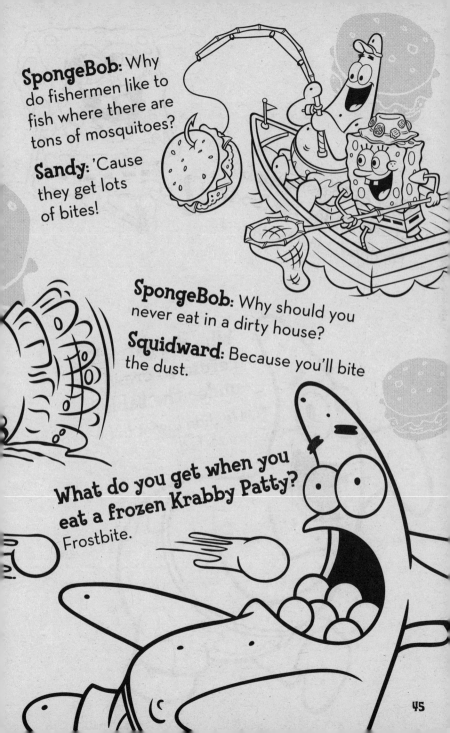

SpongeBob: Why should you never eat in a dirty house?

Squidward: Because you'll bite the dust.

What do you get when you eat a frozen Krabby Patty?

Frostbite.

Why did SpongeBob crawl under his food?

He doesn't like to overeat.

Why did Patrick refuse to crawl under the table?

He didn't want to be underfed.

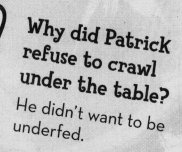

What did SpongeBob say to the Krabby Patty?

"Pleased to eat you!"

What did the Krabby Patties say when they saw their friend in Patrick's hands?

"What's eating him?"

SpongeBob: What do you call a huge lizard that only eats in the evening?

Patrick: A dinnersaur.

Squidward: Did the spatula decide to catch the patty or drop it?

SpongeBob: It left it up in the air.

SpongeBob: Why did the customer step on his check?

Squidward: He wanted to foot the bill.

Squidward: Knock-knock.

Customer: Who's there?

Squidward: Men.

Customer: Men who?

Squidward: Menu, or are you ready to order?

Mr. Krabs: What's the difference between a wiener and someone who grabs all the spots?

SpongeBob: One's a hotdog and the other's a dot hog.

Mrs. Puff: Which fruit is the saddest?

SpongeBob: The blueberry.

Sandy: What did you lose at the Chum Bucket?

SpongeBob: My appetite.

CHUM BUCKET

SpongeBob: How did Patrick get food all over the mirror?

Squidward: He was trying to feed his face.

Patrick: What happened when the patty met the bun?

SpongeBob: It was lunch at first sight.

SpongeBob: What do you get when you cross a gull and a swallow?

Sandy: A sea gulp.

Patrick: Which part of the ocean is the thirstiest?

SpongeBob: The Gulf of Mexico.

SpongeBob: Knock-knock.

Customer: Who's there?

SpongeBob: Goblet.

Customer: Goblet who?

SpongeBob: Gobble it down—it's a Krabby Patty!

How did the Krabby Patty feel when Squidward left him on the grill too long?

It really burned him up.

Why did Patrick take percussion lessons?

Mr. Krabs told him to drum up new business.

JELLYFISH JAM

Is it hard to guess Patrick's favorite dessert?

No, it's a piece of cake.

FRUITCAKE

Why did SpongeBob eat the Mystery Patty from the top down?

He wanted to get to the bottom of it.

Mr. Krabs: What did the restaurant owner say when the fisherman brought him free fish?

Squidward: "What's the catch?"

What's the difference between a mini Krabby Patty and the sound a duck with a cold makes?

One's a quick snack and the other's a sick quack.

SpongeBob: Why did the frozen boy patty throw himself at the frozen girl patty?

Sandy: He wanted to break the ice.

Mr. Krabs: Why did you paint squares on the customer?

Patrick: Uh, because he said, "Check, please."

Why did SpongeBob throw paint during his fry cook's exam?

He wanted to pass with flying colors.

Patrick: Why can't boiling pots be spies?

SpongeBob: They always blow their covers.

Why did SpongeBob jump over the eating area?

Mr. Krabs told him to clear the table.

SpongeBob: Why did the soup refuse to leave the pot?

Sandy: It was chicken.

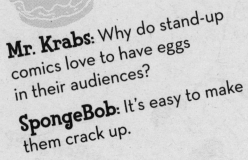

Mr. Krabs: Why do stand-up comics love to have eggs in their audiences?

SpongeBob: It's easy to make them crack up.

Why did Patrick bring a shovel to the Krusty Krab?
SpongeBob told him to dig in.

SpongeBob: How did the water feel after it washed the dishes?

Squidward: Drained.

What happened after Squidward said he'd never, ever eat alphabet soup?

He ate his words.

Patrick: How did the pancake's comedy act go over?

SpongeBob: It fell flat.

Patrick: How did that leave the pancake?

SpongeBob: Flat broke.

Why does Patrick fill his house with bread in the winter?

So it'll be nice and toasty.

Why did SpongeBob train a mouse to clean the Krusty Krab?

He wanted it to be squeaky clean.

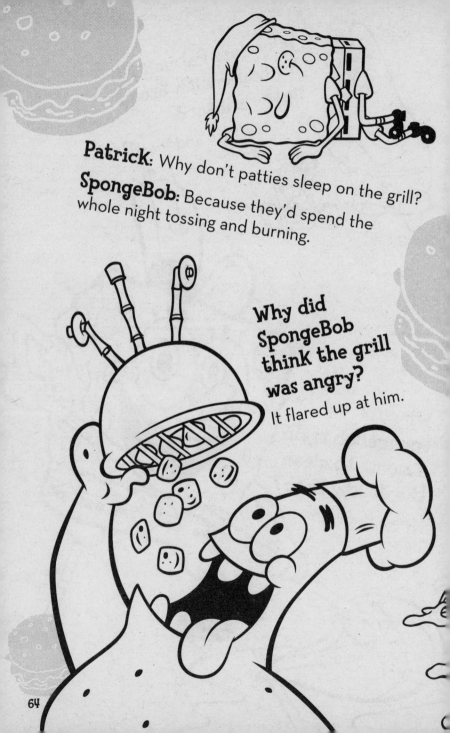

Patrick: Why don't patties sleep on the grill?

SpongeBob: Because they'd spend the whole night tossing and burning.

Why did SpongeBob think the grill was angry?

It flared up at him.

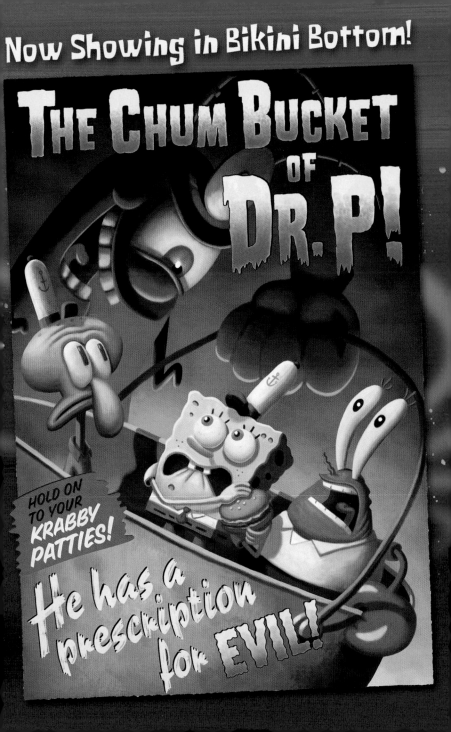

YOU WILL BE FLIPPED BY...
THE SPATULA
Shock by shock...
you will FEEL the
GRILLING
terror!
featuring
SPONGEBOB
SQUAREPANTS
SQUIDWARD
TENTACLES
MISTER
KRABS
in a
GREASY SPOON
SCREENSTAGING
ARE YOU READY
FOR WHAT THIS
IMPLEMENT OF ILL
IS SERVING UP?!

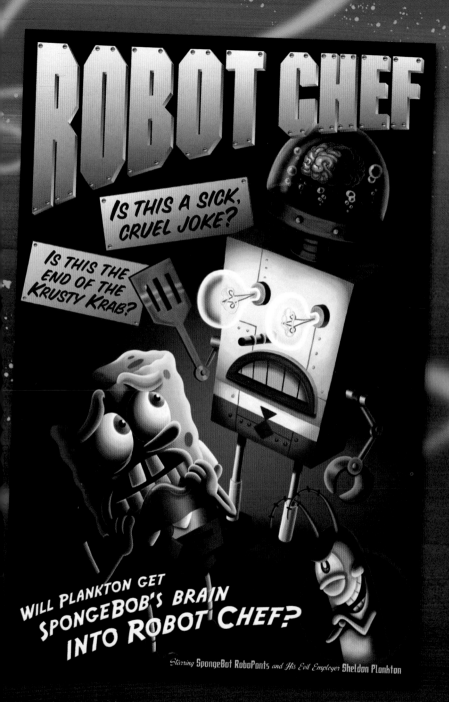

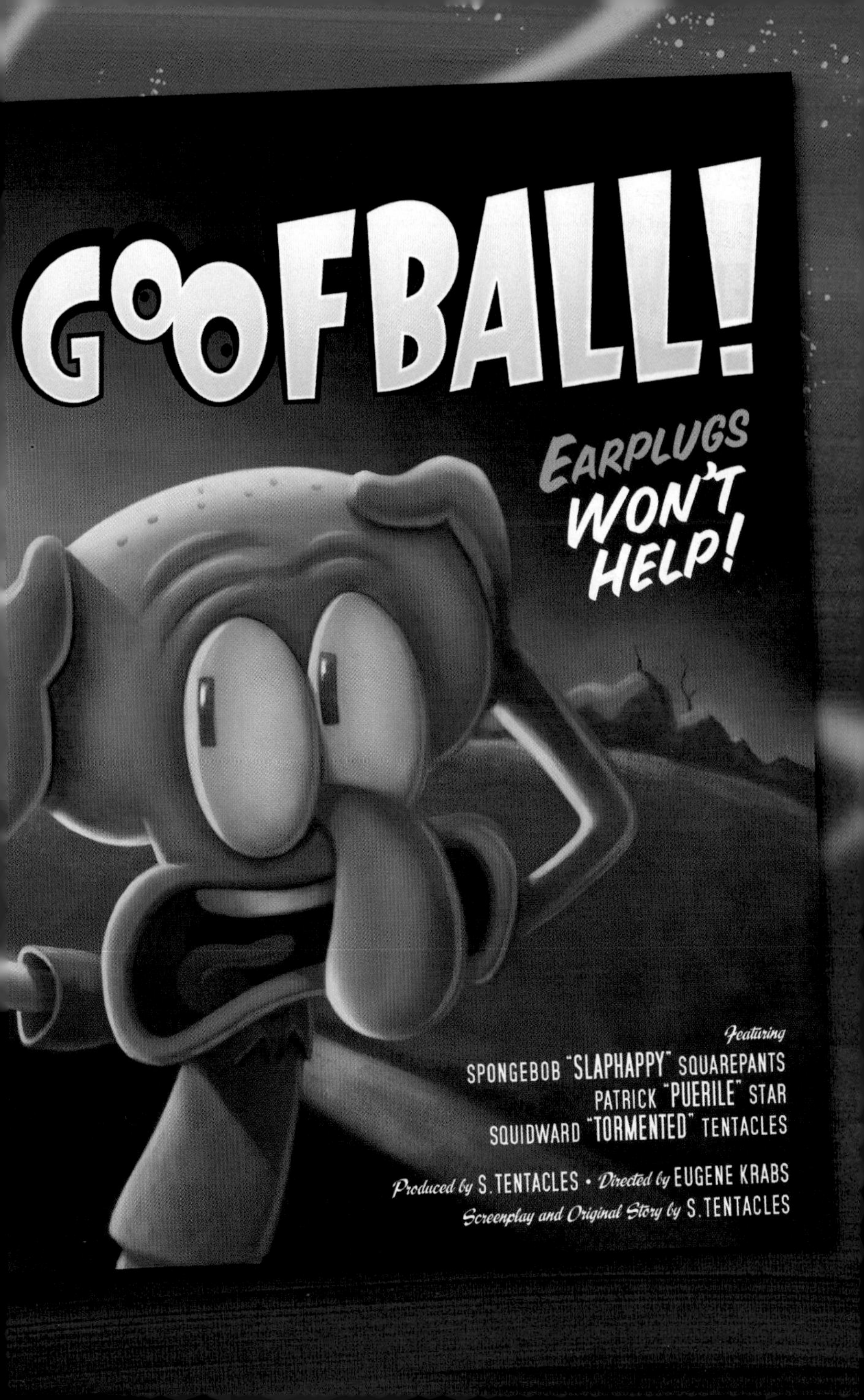
GOOFBALL!
EARPLUGS WON'T HELP!
Featuring
SPONGEBOB "SLAPHAPPY" SQUAREPANTS
PATRICK "PUERILE" STAR
SQUIDWARD "TORMENTED" TENTACLES
Produced by S. TENTACLES • Directed by EUGENE KRABS
Screenplay and Original Story by S. TENTACLES

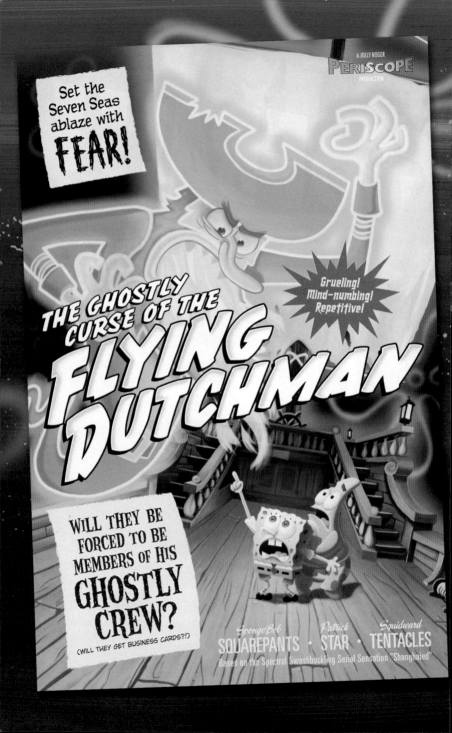

HE REPLACED
HIS HAND WITH A
RUSTY
SPATULA!
THE HASH-SLINGING
SLASHER
NOW
THIS GHOST
RETURNS TO REAP HIS
HORRIBLE REVENGE!

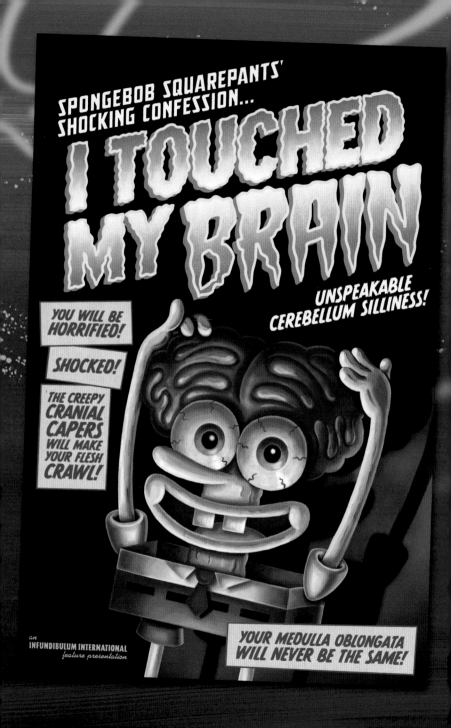

Pearl: Why didn't the ketchup tell the mustard how he felt about her?

SpongeBob: His feelings were all bottled up.

Mr. Krabs: How did the ice cream react to leaving the freezer?

Squidward: It had a total meltdown.

SpongeBob: How did the napkin do in the poker game?

Squidward: It folded.

SpongeBob: What do you get when you cross a bird with a chili?

Squidward: A woodpepper.

Why did SpongeBob tie a rope to the seat and lift it to the ceiling?

Mr. Krabs told him to pull up a chair.

Pearl: Why was the pepper exhausted?

Mrs. Puff: Because it had been put through the mill.

Why did Mr. Krabs put all his money in the freezer?

Because he wanted cold cash.

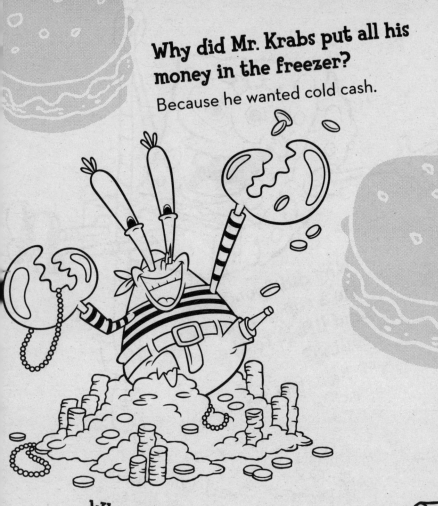

Why was the patty grouchy?

It got up on the wrong side of the bread.

Patrick: How did the milk shake feel about his time in the blender?

SpongeBob: He had mixed feelings about it.

What's Plankton's favorite kind of bread?

Shortbread.

Sandy: When does butter do its best?

SpongeBob: When it's on a roll.

What did Patrick say to the customer when he filled in for Squidward?

"May I taste your order?"

Mr. Krabs: How did the onion feel about being sliced?

SpongeBob: It really got under his skin.

SpongeBob: When does food make you itch?

Patrick: When you make it from scratch.

How does SpongeBob say good-bye to the patties when he leaves work?

"Spatulater!"

Why did SpongeBob toss a sandwich at Sandy on her birthday?

He wanted to throw her a surprise patty.

Why did SpongeBob put a circle of Krusty Krab sandwiches around his house?

He wanted to have an outdoor patty-o.

What do they call a stall in the Krusty Krab restroom?

A Krabby Potty.

Knock-Knock.

Who's there?

Stan.

Stan who?

Stan in line to order, please.

Knock-Knock.

Who's there?

Betty.

Betty who?

Bet he orders another Krabby Patty.

Knock-Knock.

Who's there?

Al.

Al who?

Al have a double Krabby Patty with cheese.

Knock-knock.
Who's there?
Donna.
Donna who?
Don a uniform before you start work.

Which big, mean fish bakes the best bread?
The Great Wheat Shark.

Why did SpongeBob jump up on the stove?
He wanted to play King of the Grill.

How would SpongeBob like working in a ship's kitchen?

It'd be right up his galley.

SpongeBob: What do you call a tortilla filled with ice?

Sandy: A brrr-ito.

SpongeBob: What do chickens eat when they wake up?

Sandy: Peckfast.

Why did Patrick attach four tires and a steering wheel to the table?

Because Mr. Krabs told him to bus it.

Mr. Krabs: What kind of cup is impossible to drink from?

Squidward: A hiccup.

Sandy: Why did the piece of corn try to join the army?

Squidward: Because he had been a kernel.

Patrick: What do ghosts order with their Krabby Patties?

SpongeBob: French frights.

Why did SpongeBob put a barbecue grill on the roof of his house?

He wanted to raise the steaks.

Sandy: Where do vegetables go to kiss?

SpongeBob: The mushroom.

Why did Patrick throw the T-bone in a blender?

He wanted to make a chocolate milk steak.

Why did Patrick try to have a conversation with a can of beans?

Because he'd heard there was a story called "Jack and the Beans Talk."

SpongeBob: What do ducks eat for lunch?

Patrick: Quackaroni and cheese.

Sandy: What's green and comes on a bun?

Plankton: A hambooger.

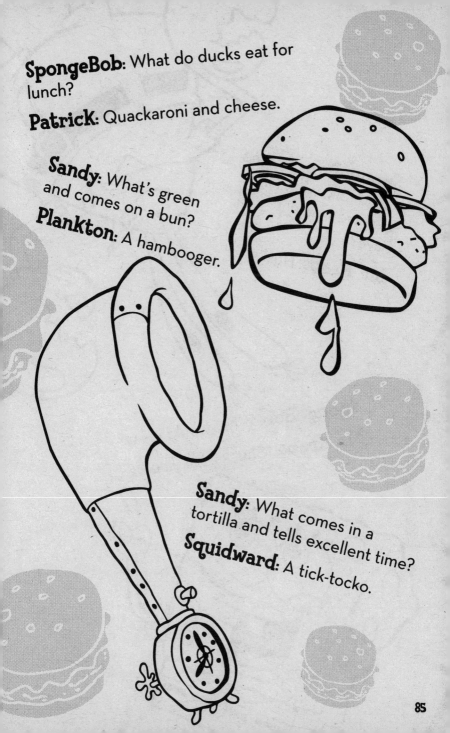

Sandy: What comes in a tortilla and tells excellent time?

Squidward: A tick-tocko.

SpongeBob: If corn could talk, what kind of voice would it have?

Mr. Krabs: Husky.

SpongeBob: What would it say?

Mr. Krabs: "Shucks, I'm all ears."

SpongeBob: What did the waiter say to the frog?

Squidward: "You want flies with that?"

What did SpongeBob say when he ran out of cabbage?

"That's the last slaw."

Why did SpongeBob practice his karate at the Krusty Krab?

He thought he was supposed to punch in and punch out.

Where do crabs take classes?

Claw school.

What's Mr. Krabs's favorite chore?

Taking out the cash.

Does SpongeBob have a good time at work?

Yes, he's the life of the patty.

What do Krabby Patties and long hair have in common?

They both fit in a bun.

Patrick: What do jellyfish eat for breakfast?

SpongeBob: Floatmeal!

SpongeBob: What has two big claws and is very messy?

Patrick: A slobster!

What happened when Patrick tried to sketch a picture of his brain?

He drew a blank.

What kind of fish hates to wear clothes?

Bare-acudas.

Why did SpongeBob visit the Arctic Ocean?

He just wanted to chill.

Mermaid Man: How did the other students do on Mrs. Puff's test?

Barnacle Boy: They sailed through it.

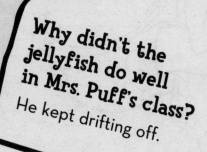

Why didn't the jellyfish do well in Mrs. Puff's class?
He kept drifting off.

Why won't SpongeBob drive to Patrick's house?
He doesn't want to rock the boat.

What happened when SpongeBob ate mashed potatoes in Mrs. Puff's class?

He got a lump in his boat.

Patrick: Do you like barnacles?

SpongeBob: They're growing on me.

What did Mrs. Puff do at the end of SpongeBob's lesson?

She went on a long inflation.

Patrick: What's Plankton's favorite dessert?

SpongeBob: Shortcake.

If Patrick's best friend were a dessert, what kind would he be?

Sponge cake.

Why would Mr. Krabs like to be a bowl of chocolate ice cream?

Because it's very rich.

Patrick: Who haunts the seven seas but never vacuums?

SpongeBob: The Flying Dustman!

Mermaid Man: What does it take to get into a fish choir?

Barnacle Boy: You have to be able to carry a tuna.

Why did Patrick pull the ship with a rope?

He'd heard it was a tugboat.

Where would
SpongeBob live after
an earthquake?

In a pineapple
upside-down house.

What do you call someone
who just sits around blowing
into a shell?

A conch potato!

Why didn't SpongeBob's
pants fall down during
the hurricane?

He was saved by the belt.

Sandy: Why didn't the boy penguin ask the girl penguin out on a date?

SpongeBob: He got cold feet.

How is Sandy able to get around Bikini Bottom without getting wet?

She has her dry-fur's license.

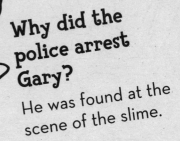

Why did the police arrest Gary?

He was found at the scene of the slime.

Knock-knock.

Who's there?

Hatch.

Hatch who?

Gesundheit!

Knock-knock.

Who's there?

Claire.

Claire who?

Clarinets sound beautiful, don't they?

Why does Mr. Krabs have so many clocks in his house?

Because time is money.

Why does Mr. Krabs like to mop up?

Because inside every bucket, there's a buck.

Why did SpongeBob put his ear to the cash register?

Because Mr. Krabs told him, "Money talks."

Was Mr. Krabs mad
when SpongeBob
dropped the butter?

No, he let it slide.

What do you call Mr. Krabs
when he's holding a coin?

A penny-pincher.

How does SpongeBob get exercise?

He does deep-sea bends.

Why did the quilt refuse to go to Bikini Bottom?

She didn't want to be a wet blanket.

What does SpongeBob sleep in?

His under-square.

Where do sea cows sleep at night?

In the barn-acle.

Squidward: Why do starfish get up in the middle of the night?

SpongeBob: They have to twinkle.

How do you save jellyfish from drowning?

Throw them some life preserves.

Why couldn't Patrick understand what the jellyfish was saying?

It was way over his head.

Why did SpongeBob toss the sandwich at Patrick?

He wanted to throw him a surprise patty.

SpongeBob: What has horns, four legs, and is made out of soap?

Sandy: A bubbalo!

When is SpongeBob like a battery?

When he gets all charged up!

Why doesn't SpongeBob go to the barber?

He doesn't like to cut corners.

Why do SpongeBob and Sandy surf so well together?

They're on the same wavelength.

What did Sandy say when she finished gathering acorns?

"That's all, oaks!"

How does Sandy feel about SpongeBob?

She's nuts about him!

What's SpongeBob's favorite last-minute Halloween costume?

Swiss cheese.

Why do clams and mussels not like to share?

Because they're shellfish.

Pearl: Did you hear the one about the banana that got sunburned?

Patrick: No.

Pearl: It began to peel. Did you hear the one about the lunchmeat?

Patrick: No.

Pearl: It's a bunch of baloney. Did you hear the one about the stale cookie?

Pearl: Yeah, it was really crummy.

Pearl: What did the mayonnaise say to the refrigerator?

Patrick: Please close the door. I'm dressing.

What kind of lettuce did they serve on the *Titanic?*

Iceberg.

What happens when you ask shellfish personal questions?

They clam up.

What kind of fruit do sailors like most?

Naval oranges.

Mrs. Puff: What fruit conquered the world?

SpongeBob: Alexander the Grape.

SpongeBob: What do you call fake spaghetti?

Squidward: Mock-aroni.

If a tomato and a lettuce had a race, which would win?

Lettuce, because it's always a head.

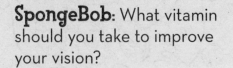

SpongeBob: What vitamin should you take to improve your vision?

Squidward: Vitamin See.

Why did Patrick take a dozen eggs to the gym?

He wanted them to get some eggs-ercise.

Why did Patrick throw sticks of margarine out the window?

He wanted to see butter fly.

What do you call SpongeBob when he sings and drinks soda at the same time?

A pop singer.

What's the smallest room in the world?

A mushroom.

What does SpongeBob's daily diet consist of?

Three square meals.

Why does Patrick like to talk to a cornfield?

Because it's all ears.

What sandwich is always scared?

A chicken sandwich.

SpongeBob: What do you give a lemon when it needs help?

Sandy: Lemon-aid.

What did Patrick say to the pickle?

"You're dill-icious!"

Why did Patrick want a job in the salt and pepper factory?

He was hoping to find seasonal work.

What do sea monsters eat?

Fish and ships.

SpongeBob: Why are tomatoes the slowest vegetable?

Mr. Krabs: They're always trying to ketchup.

Mrs. Puff: I asked you to write a composition on cheese yesterday. You didn't hand anything in. Why not?

SpongeBob: The tip of my pen kept getting clogged with cheese.

SpongeBob: Mr. Krabs, do you know how to make a lobster roll?

Mr. Krabs: Sure. Just take a lobster to the top of a hill and push!

Mr. Krabs: SpongeBob, why is it taking you so long to fill the salt shakers?

SpongeBob: It's really hard getting the salt through the little holes on top.

Patrick: How much is a soda?

Mr. Krabs: A dollar.

Patrick: How much is a refill?

Mr. Krabs: It's free.

Patrick: Well then, I'll take the refill.

Sandy: SpongeBob, tell me the joke about the butter.

SpongeBob: No, you'd only spread it around.

Sandy: Then tell me the one about the egg.

SpongeBob: Oh, that one will crack you up.

Sandy: Did I tell you the one about the banana peel?

SpongeBob: No.

Sandy: It must have slipped my mind.

SpongeBob: You should go wash your face. I can tell what you had for breakfast today.

Patrick: Oh, yeah? What did I have for breakfast today?

SpongeBob: Oatmeal.

Patrick: Sorry, you're wrong. That was yesterday.

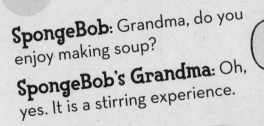

SpongeBob: Grandma, do you enjoy making soup?

SpongeBob's Grandma: Oh, yes. It is a stirring experience.

Cracked-Up Cookbooks

Sweet Treats
by Candy Kane

Picnic Favorites
by Frank Furter

The Big Book of Pizza Toppings
by Anne Chovey, Tom Maito, and Mead Ball

Double-Fudge Cakes
and Other High-Calorie Desserts
by Rich N. Faddening

The Raw Onion Cookbook
by Wendy U. Weepalot

Seven-Course Meals
and Other Feasts
by Phil Mabelly

Nutty Knock-Knocks

Knock-Knock.

Who's there?

Pecan.

Pecan who?

Pecan someone your own size!

Knock-Knock.

Who's there?

Justin.

Justin who?

Justin time for Krabby Patties.

Knock-knock.

Who's there?

Doughnut.

Doughnut who?

Doughnut open till Christmas.

Knock-knock.

Who's there?

Duncan.

Duncan who?

Duncan cookies in milk is yummy.

Knock-knock.

Who's there?

Ice-cream soda.

Ice-cream soda who?

Ice-scream soda people in Bikini Bottom can hear me.

Knock-Knock.

Who's there?

Lettuce.

Lettuce who?

Lettuce stop telling these jokes already!